THE MAZE OF THE SPHINX

THE MAZE OF THE SPHINX

By Tracey West

Random House 🏠 New York

Manufactured under licence granted to AMEET Sp. z o.o. by the LEGO Group.

AMEET Sp. z o.o.
Nowe Sady 6, 94-102 Łódź—Poland
ameet@ameet.eu
www.ameet.eu

www.LEGO.com

Published in the United States by Random House Children's Books, a division of Penguin Random House LLC, 1745 Broadway, New York, NY 10019, and in Canada by Penguin Random House Canada Limited, Toronto. Random House and the colophon are registered trademarks of Penguin Random House LLC.

rhcbooks.com

ISBN 978-0-593-43072-9 (trade) — ISBN 978-0-593-43073-6 (lib. bdg.)
ISBN 978-0-593-43074-3 (ebook)

Printed in the United States of America

10 9 8 7 6 5 4 3 2 1

First Edition 2022

CONTENTS

Prologue 1

Chapter 1: Valley of the Sphinx 7

Chapter 2: Nobody Leaves! 17

Chapter 3: Pick a Door! 23

Chapter 4: Soldiers in the Sand 31

Chapter 5: Shezada 45

Chapter 6: The Smart-Mouthed Sphinx 59

Chapter 7: The Mirror of Dread 71

Chapter 8: Just a Little Bite 83

Chapter 9: Battle of the Ghouls 97

Chapter 10: The Blue Warriors 109

Chapter 11: One Wish 119

Epilogue 129

Glossary 133

Prologue

Cole patted his stomach. "Kai, are we getting close to the restaurant? I'm hungry."

The ninja and Master Wu were on their way to try a new barbecue shop in Ninjago City.

"We're almost there. It's just a block past the Explorers' Club," Kai answered.

They were approaching the club—a fancy building surrounded by a black iron fence.

"That place is filled with stuffy old guys with too many rules," Nya complained. "The last time Lloyd, Zane, and I were here, they wouldn't let us enter. We had to sneak in and—"

wHoosH!

A huge stream of orange flame shot from the front door of the Explorers' Club.

"Fire in the club!" yelled Lloyd, the leader of the ninja. "There could be people inside!" He pulled open the iron gate and crashed through a window. The other ninja followed him.

They found Cecil Putnam, the club manager, cowering behind the front desk.

"Be careful!" he warned. "The Sphinx statue is out of control!"

"What's a Sphinx?" Jay asked.

"The only thing in the room shooting fire from its eyes!" Cecil snapped.

A large stone statue stood on a platform in the front hall of the Explorers' Club, behind three flaming torches. The statue had a mouth full of sharp teeth, a headdress that looked like a lion's mane, and glowing red eyes.

"You mean this one? But it's not spitting fire right now," Jay pointed out.

"Just wait," Cecil replied. "Three . . . two . . . one . . . DUCK!"

Whoosh!
A stream of fire shot from the statue's mouth!

"On it!" Nya cried, and she held out her arms toward the statue. Shimmering blue water flowed from her hands, and a huge wave splashed over the fire—and onto Kai.

"Hey! I spent thirty minutes getting my hair perfect today!" he wailed.

"Based on the intervals between flames, we have approximately *thirty seconds* to prevent another fiery blast," said Zane. He somersaulted through the air and touched the Sphinx with his hand. A thick layer of ice immediately froze the statue's head.

"Good work, ninja!" Master Wu praised them.

Cecil stood up. "Thank you," he said. "The statue is malfunctioning! It rose from the floor and started shooting fire, and I didn't even press the button."

He ran over to the statue and slid open a hidden panel on the base. Then he pressed some switches.

"There, I've deactivated it," Cecil reported. "We'll have a technician take a look at it once the ice melts."

"Don't you think it's foolish to keep something so dangerous in the middle of a crowded city?" Lloyd asked.

"Compared to a real Sphinx, this one wasn't so dangerous," said Master Wu.

Nya raised an eyebrow. "Hold on, Master Wu. Are you saying that Sphinxes actually exist?" she asked.

Master Wu nodded.

"Well, what's more dangerous than something that blasts fire every minute?" Jay asked.

"Power and deceit can often be more dangerous than fire," Master Wu replied. "My brother, Garmadon, and I encountered one on the quest we took when we were younger—when our father sent us to find a special tea plant that would help cure Garmadon's growing darkness."

"Ooh, another story about the Spinjitzu brothers!" Jay cried happily. "Master Wu, you have to tell us everything that happened."

Cole's stomach growled. "Can you tell us at the barbecue restaurant?"

"Certainly," Master Wu replied. "I am hungry, too."

They left the Explorers' Club, sloshing through the puddles of water on the floor on their way out.

Cecil gazed around the room. "Hey! You've left quite a mess here!" he called after them, but the ninja were well on their way. . . .

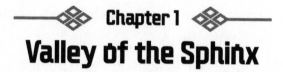

Chapter 1
Valley of the Sphinx

"Which way do we go?" Wu wondered out loud.

Wu and his brother, Garmadon, were on a journey to the Northern Ocean to find a special tea plant. It was a long way to go for some tea, but their father had insisted. Garmadon had been bitten by an evil serpent, and the First Spinjitzu Master was worried that evil had poisoned his son. The tea, he believed, would cure Garmadon.

The night before, they'd taken shelter from the rain in a cave. They'd disturbed a bat colony, which chased them deep into the cave, and they'd gotten lost. After a restless night, they'd loaded up their packs and taken a few steps—only to find themselves surrounded by tunnels. Neither brother was sure how to get back to where they'd come in.

"I don't think it matters which one we go through," Garmadon said. "Let's just pick one! I'm thirsty, and we need to refill out water pouches."

"But what if one of these tunnels leads to something dangerous?" Wu asked.

"We're ninja! We'll fight it!" Garmadon replied. Then he headed down one of the tunnels without waiting for another word from Wu.

After five minutes of jogging through the dark tunnel, a bright light hit their eyes. They emerged into a desert.

Wu and Garmadon stared in disbelief at the village spread out before them. Dozens of block-shaped, straw-colored homes were scattered across the sand. A marketplace running through the village featured stalls with colorful canopies. People streamed into the marketplace, carrying baskets filled with fabric, bread, and fruit.

And towering over it all was an enormous pyramid made of smooth, gleaming black stone.

"A pyramid?" Wu asked. "This is *definitely* not the way we came. In fact, I'd say that this is a pretty weird development."

"Don't be a worrywart, Wu," Garmadon said, and Wu scowled. Wu knew his brother was probably just as confused as he was by this, but he would never show it. "At least we found civilization," Garmadon continued. "I bet we can get some good food here. And maybe one of those people in the funny hats knows how to get to the Northern Ocean."

"Funny hats?" Wu asked, and then he noticed—all of the villagers were wearing black hats shaped like the giant pyramid.

That's odd, Wu thought, and he jogged ahead to catch up to his brother, who was already talking to one of the hat-wearers.

"Hello!" Garmadon greeted the villager. "My brother and I have come from very far. What is this place?"

"Welcome, strangers, to the Valley of the Sphinx," the man said. He wore light-colored robes as well as his hat, and a friendly smile on his face. "I am Sage."

"Thanks," Wu replied. "I'm Wu, and this is Garmadon. Um, where is that, exactly? Are we anywhere near the Northern Ocean?"

"And what's with the giant pyramid?" Garmadon asked.

Sage's dark eyes twinkled. "So many questions," he said. "Come with me, please, and I will answer you over some tea."

"Speaking of tea, do you know anything about a special tea that grows on the shores of the Northern Ocean?" Garmadon asked as they made their way through the marketplace.

Sage shook his head. "I have never left the valley," he said. Then he led them inside a stall selling baskets filled with baked treats. A woman dressed in the same hat and robes as Sage was helping a customer. She turned and looked at them.

"Is there tea, Mina?" Sage asked.

The woman nodded. "I just made a pot. Welcome, strangers."

They sat on a colorful rug with Sage, who poured tea into two shiny black cups. Both boys forgot about their questions as he passed them a plate filled with cakes, glistening with honey.

"Thanks for your hospitality," Wu said, after filling his belly. "Can you please tell us exactly where we are?"

Sage shrugged. "Is that important? We are in the Valley of the Sphinx. We are born here, and we never leave here. The Sphinx provides for our needs."

"What's a Sphinx?" Wu asked.

"She is a marvelous creature who lives inside the pyramid and grants wishes," the man replied. "But when she is displeased, she sends out her beetle warriors to punish us."

Wu raised an eyebrow. "And how do you please this creature?"

Sage pointed to his pyramid-shaped hat. "We wear these to keep the Sphinx happy," he explained. "They must be worn for the Please Don't Destroy Us ritual, which we perform three times a day."

"Does the Sphinx ever come out of the pyramid herself?" Wu asked.

"Never," Sage replied. "And none who have seen her have survived to tell the tale. Everything we know, we know from the ancient scrolls."

Garmadon frowned. "Do you mean to tell me your whole lives revolve around pleasing some monster who might not even be real? Why don't you all rise up and fight?"

Sage shook his head. "Shhhhh! Don't let the Sphinx hear you."

Garmadon shrugged. "I'm not afraid of any Sphinx. Besides, if she grants wishes, maybe we should pay her a visit."

The villager shook his hat-topped head. "It is not worth the risk, trust me. It is too easy to make the Sphinx angry."

"We don't have time to talk to a mythical magical wish-granter, anyway," Wu said. "Is there another village near here, where maybe—"

But Garmadon had jumped up and was jogging off again. Wu sighed.

"I apologize for my brother's bad manners," he said. "Thank you, Sage and Mina."

Then he took off after Garmadon.

We can't seem to agree on anything lately, he thought. *Then again, Garmadon and I have never agreed on much!*

"How do you get in here, anyway?" Garmadon was asking, feeling the smooth stone of the pyramid.

Suddenly, the stone slid to one side. "A doorway!" Garmadon cried, and he stepped inside.

Wu groaned and followed his brother. "Come on, Garmadon. I know these villagers might be telling us a fairytale, but what if they're not? Even if the Sphinx isn't real, those beetle warriors might be."

They had entered a small, square room with smooth black walls. The door slid shut behind them. Wu pushed against it, but it wouldn't budge. He gave it a kick.

"We're trapped! I told you this was a bad idea," Wu snapped.

"There's always a way out," Garmadon said confidently. "Anyway, aren't you even a little curious to see this Sphinx? Think about it. We could wish for the tea and go back home. No more wandering around Ninjago."

Wu paused. "You do have a point," he agreed. "Maybe we could even wish that you'd never gotten bit by the Great Devourer in the first place!"

Garmadon's face clouded. "I don't know why you and Father think that was such a big deal. It was just one bite. And I haven't changed. I'm still—"

wHoosH!

A trapdoor opened underneath their feet!

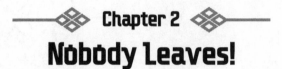

Chapter 2
Nobody Leaves!

"Whoooooooaaaaaaaaaa!"

Wu and Garmadon plummeted through the trap door into darkness. Their ninja instincts kicked in immediately, and they both prepared their bodies for a safe landing—and whatever opponent might be waiting for them at the bottom.

The drop wasn't far, and they both landed on their feet on a stone floor. Fiery torches suddenly lit up on the surrounding walls.

They were in a cavernous room almost completely filled by an enormous creature. It looked like a lion, with a big cat's golden fur, paws, and tail. But its face looked like a woman's, with glowing red eyes and

sharp teeth. Jeweled wings sprouted from its back. A gold collar glittered around its neck, and a blue and gold headdress crowned it like a lion's mane.

"WHO DARES TO ENTER THE PYRAMID OF THE SPHINX?" the creature asked in a thunderous female voice.

Garmadon nudged Wu. "Well, I guess the Sphinx is real after all," he said in a whisper.

Wu cleared his throat. "We don't want to bother you," he called to the Sphinx. "If you could just show us the way out, we would—"

"Actually, we heard you grant wishes," Garmadon said. "I'd like one, please."

Oh no, here comes trouble! Wu thought.

"WHERE ARE YOUR HATS?" the Sphinx asked.

"Hats?" Garmadon repeated. "My brother's wearing a hat. . . . Oh, you mean like the villagers. We're not from here. We are Wu and Garmadon, sons of the First Spinjitzu Master."

"Hmmm," the Sphinx said, lowering her voice. "It would be foolish to anger the First Spinjitzu Master, and I am not foolish. For that reason, I shall spare you. But in order to leave, you must find your way through the maze inside this pyramid and return to my chamber alive. If you succeed, I will grant you one wish, as I do all who accept my challenge."

"A maze?" Garmadon asked. "That doesn't sound so tough."

Wu stepped in front of him. "Um, oh great Sphinx, we don't really need a wish. We'd rather be on our way. Can't you just let us leave?"

"NOBODY LEAVES THIS PYRAMID EXCEPT THROUGH THE MAZE," the Sphinx roared. "Also, nobody has ever survived the maze. That's why the reward is so remarkable."

I don't have a good feeling about this, Wu thought. "It sounds like we don't have a choice," he said out loud.

"YOU DO NOT!"

Then the floor opened up underneath them, and they fell into the maze.

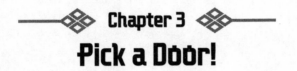

Chapter 3
Pick a Door!

"Not agaaaaaaaaaaaaaaaaaaaaaain!" the brothers wailed as they fell.

Their ninja training saved them. They twisted in the air and landed on their feet in a dark, narrow room.

"I thought this was supposed to be a maze," Garmadon complained. "How are we supposed to find our way through it if we can't even see?"

Suddenly, torches lit up on the wall immediately to their left and right. Each torch lit up a carved stone door with a golden handle.

Whooooosh! One by one, torches lit up down the hallway, revealing dozens more doors . . . so many that Wu couldn't guess how many there were.

"This must be the start of the maze," Wu reasoned. "I guess we have to accept the Sphinx's challenge whether we want to or not."

He gazed up, at the dark abyss they'd just fallen from. "I bet we could use Spinjitzu to get back up there. Then we could battle the Sphinx and get on our way."

"But *then* we wouldn't get a wish," Garmadon pointed out. "I mean, haven't you had enough of this road-trip-to-nowhere? One wish and we could be back home, with things the way they always were."

Wu paused. He didn't mind the journey with his brother so much, but the idea that the wish could somehow erase the bite of the Great Devourer intrigued him. Deep down, he worried about his brother and how the bite was affecting him. It would be such a relief to let go of that worry.

"Well . . . ," Wu said slowly.

Garmadon grinned. "Come on, let's pick a door and get started."

He walked to the nearest door, but Wu jumped in front of him.

"Wait!" Wu cried. "This has to be some kind of trick. There could be dangers behind these doors."

"Calm down, brother," Garmadon replied. "We've got to start somewhere, don't we?"

Garmadon pushed Wu aside and pulled on the handle to open the door.

"OOOOOOEEEEEEEEEEEEE!"

A bloodcurdling scream came from behind the door, and Garmadon quickly closed it.

"Maybe not that one," Garmadon said, and he jogged down the corridor to find another door.

Wu followed him. "Garmadon listen to me! Maybe we should—"

His brother opened another door, and a shower of spears shot out. Garmadon tucked and somersaulted, avoiding them.

"Definitely not that one," he said, as Wu quickly shut the door.

Garmadon ran to a third door on the right, and Wu ninja-flipped and landed ahead of him. Garmadon reached for the door to the left instead.

A cloud of green smoke puffed out, and a terrible stench filled their noses.

"Ugh! Rotten eggs!" Wu cried.

"Ugh! Your armpits!" Garmadon teased, and he shut the door.

"Very funny," Wu said. "*Now* will you admit that—"

But Garmadon had already jumped to another door. This time, nothing shot out.

Wu couldn't believe it. "Does it lead to a passageway?"

"Nope," Garmadon answered, shutting the door. "There's just another wall behind it. A dud. It doesn't lead anywhere."

GROOOAAAAAAAAN

A loud grinding sound filled the air, and the stone ceiling slowly began to lower toward them.

"We're going to be squashed like bugs!" Wu cried. "When you opened the door, it must have triggered this!"

Garmadon looked down at his feet. "Okay, I guess you were right about these doors being dangerous," he admitted. "So what's your plan?"

"What's *my* plan?" Wu yelled. "You're the one who got us into this mess."

"Yeah, I get it!" Garmadon shouted, and Wu heard the panic in his brother's voice. "Um, what if we try opening some more doors?"

"Are you kidding me?" Wu shouted back.

The ceiling above their heads inched closer toward them. Wu took a deep breath.

Think, Wu, he told himself. *There's got to be a trick to getting out of here . . . maybe some kind of marks on the doors?*

The doors were blank and smooth, but then Wu noticed something. The floor at their feet was made of stones, and each stone had a letter on it. But the letters didn't seem to spell anything. Unless . . .

"Garmadon, do you remember Father's lessons on code-breaking?" Wu asked.

"Sure," Garmadon replied. "They were much less boring than his history lessons. But is this really a time to be discussing childhood memories?"

"Those lessons are our way out of here!" Wu said. "Follow me to the start of the corridor!"

He took off running.

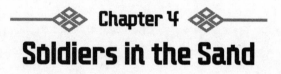

Chapter 4
Soldiers in the Sand

The ceiling groaned, inching closer to their heads, as Wu and Garmadon reached the start of the corridor. Wu gazed down at the floor.

"Look, the letters don't make sense," he said. He read the letters aloud, going across the first row of stones. "*K-X-Y-E-Ó-L-E-B-D-P* . . . it's got to be a code!"

"Don't you think the letters are scrambled?" Garmadon wondered.

"They could be," Wu guessed, as the ceiling groaned again. "But unscrambling all these letters would take too much time. I'm thinking the code might be every other letter. *K-Y-O-E* . . ."

"That's not it," Garmadon said. He stared at the stones. "What about every third letter? *K-E-E-P.* Keep!"

Wu nodded. "That's got to be it! Quick! Let's decode the rest!"

The brothers jumped from stone to stone as they made their way down the corridor. They ducked lower and lower as they moved, saying the words out loud as they decoded them.

"*Y-O-U-R, E-Y-E-S, O-N, T-H-E, F-L-O-O-R, T-O, L-A-N-D, A-T, T-H-E, R-I-G-H-T, D-O-O-R.* Keep your eyes on the floor to land at the right door! We got it!"

By the time they landed at the last letter—*R*—they were on their knees, and the ceiling was just inches

above their heads. Garmadon pushed the door open, and they crawled through.

Whomp! The door thudded shut behind them. Both boys froze and waited.

"No monsters. No screams," Wu remarked.

"And the ceiling isn't trying to squash us!" Garmadon cried, springing to his feet.

Wu jumped up, and the brothers high-fived.

"We did it!" Wu cheered. "We make a great team!"

"Yeah!" Garmadon agreed, but a flash of doubt clouded his brain.

Does he really mean it? Garmadon wondered. *Wu hasn't looked at me the same ever since that dumb snake bit me. And as for being a team . . . he's always trying to tell me what to do. How is that teamwork?*

Wu examined the narrow hallway. "I guess we made it into the maze," he said. "Looks like there's a turn down there."

"Might as well start trying to get back to the Sphinx," Garmadon said, and he moved past his brother.

"Don't you think we need a kind of strategy?" Wu asked. "Like, leaving a breadcrumb trail or something like that?"

"Sage and Mina's cakes barely made a dent in my belly, and we've only got one hunk of bread left. I'm not wasting those crumbs in the maze," Garmadon replied. "Anyway, that first chamber was all about surprises and dangers. The only strategy we're going to need is Spinjitzu—follow the path, fight whatever gets in our way, and we'll be good."

"Hmm," Wu said, but he didn't argue. He and Garmadon walked down the corridor. When they got to the turn, Wu slowly peered around the corner.

"Coast is clear."

"Seriously? Are you going to do that at *every* turn?" Garmadon asked. "It'll take forever to get out of this horrible place."

"At least we will get out, if we're careful," Wu countered.

They continued through the maze. Torches on the wall lit the way, but they were few and far between, and the boys' eyes adjusted to the dim light. Walking with ninja stealth, they barely made a sound as they traveled across the smooth stone.

The passageway turned right, then left, then left again, then right. Then the path ended in a T, with a choice to go either left or right.

The brothers stopped.

"Our first choice!" Garmadon announced.

"We need to think carefully. One way could lead to victory, and the other—certain doom," Wu said in a serious voice.

"Well, I'm not afraid of doom," Garmadon said. "I mean, we're the sons of the First Spinjitzu Master, having an adventure. You don't really think we'll get through this maze without a problem, do you?"

Wu sighed. "Why can't anything be easy for once?"

"It's going to be what it's going to be, and we'll be ready for whatever that is," Garmadon assured him. "So it doesn't matter which way we choose."

Wu nodded. "You're right. Let's go left!"

They made a left turn. The hallway looked the same, with no dangers in sight. The only difference was that the stone floor had turned to sand. And as they walked, the corridor grew wider.

"Looks like you made a good choice, brother," Garmadon remarked. *Figures Wu would get it right,* he thought.

That was when the warriors rose up from the ground, fully formed, in front of them. They looked to be entirely made of sand, wearing helmets, chest plates, and skirts. The spears they carried seemed to be made of metal—gleaming gold. Blank white eyes stared from their faces, and a mask covered each soldier's nose and mouth. A dozen of them stood in four lines in front of the brothers, blocking their way.

"What were you saying about a good choice?" Wu asked.

"They're made of sand. How hard can it be to defeat them?" Garmadon wondered. He launched into a Spinjitzu tornado and whirled toward the first line of warriors.

"Ninjaaaaaaaaa—"

Wham! Garmadon bounced back from the soldiers and landed next to Wu.

"They're hard as rocks!" he cried. "How are we supposed to beat them?"

Wu looked at him and smiled. "Together," he said, and he spun into a Spinjitzu tornado. Garmadon did the same, and together they slammed into one of the warriors.

The warrior tipped backward, knocking into the warrior behind him. That started a chain reaction, and two more warriors tipped over. Garmadon noticed a slight shimmer in their forms as they fell.

BAM!

Garmadon delivered a spinning kick to one of the warriors as he fell.

POOF!

The warrior dissolved into sand.

"One down!" Garmadon yelled. "Wu, you gotta get them while they're moving."

The boys spun toward another warrior, and rather than be sitting targets, the sand warriors started fighting back.

Garmadon leaned to the side to avoid a spear thrust, and then struck the warrior as he pulled back his arm.

POOF!

Another warrior dissolved.

Wu jumped over a swinging spear and landed in a somersault. He grabbed the spear from another

warrior, who gave chase. Wu spun around mid-run
and roundhouse-kicked the sand soldier.

POOF!

The two brothers whirled through the hallway,
dodging spears and attacking the warriors whenever
they moved. It wasn't long before they were standing
on top of a mound of sand, with golden spears
scattered around them.

"We did it!" Garmadon cheered.

"Maybe you're right, brother," Wu said. "We'll fight
our way out of here in no time."

The two brothers jumped off the sand mound—
and the floor opened up underneath their feet. They
plummeted into darkness.

"Reaaaaaaaaaaaaalllllllllyyyyyyyyyy?" they yelled.

This time, they collided on the way down and tumbled onto a cold floor. Garmadon tried to sit up— but felt a foot push down on his chest. He looked up to see a masked figure standing over them, with a spear pressed to Wu's throat!

Chapter 5
Shezada

The brothers leapt into action. Wu grabbed the spear and pushed their attacker aside while Garmadon jumped to his feet, adding his strength to Wu's move.

Another sand warrior? Wu wondered. But this opponent moved with skilled speed, almost ninja-like. After a graceful backflip, the attacker swiftly twirled the spear and then struck each of the brothers with the dull end before they could react.

The blow knocked both boys off their feet, but they weren't down for long. They launched into Spinjitzu tornadoes and whirled toward the attacker, who somersaulted and tried to knock them down with the spear. The strike didn't slow the boys, who stopped twirling, and blocked the masked figure on either side. Wu noticed distinctly human eyes behind the mask as the figure held out the spear defensively. His brother had the same thought at the same time.

"Wu, this isn't a sand warrior!" Garmadon called.

Wu nodded, then addressed the masked fighter. "Hey, we're trapped here, just like you! We're not your enemy!"

The attacker eyed both of them for a moment. Then they lowered the spear and took off the brown cloth that covered their head, nose, and mouth. Underneath was a long mane of black hair and the face of a young woman with dark eyes and a scar on her left cheek.

"You got past the sand warriors?" she asked. "Nobody ever gets past the sand warriors. Nobody but me, anyway."

"Yeah, well, it wasn't that hard," Garmadon said with a shrug.

The girl raised an eyebrow. "Okay, then. I'm Shezada. Sorry I attacked you, but I've been stuck in this pyramid for a few weeks and I'm on automatic fighting mode. Better follow me, and I'll explain everything. This corridor isn't safe."

Should we trust her? Wu wondered, but Garmadon didn't seem to have any doubts and was already at Shezada's heels. Wu noticed she was dressed like a desert traveler, in light-colored clothing that looked easy to move around in. Her boots had clearly carried her for many miles. And along with her spear, she had a bow and a quiver of arrows strapped to her back.

More like a warrior than a traveler, maybe, Wu guessed.

They all traveled through twists and turns, and then Shezada stopped. She slid aside a round, stone plate to reveal a hole underneath.

"Down here," she said, and she jumped down through the hole. The brothers looked at each other.

"Down again?" asked Wu, frowning.

"Why am I not surprised? At least we're *deciding* to fall through a hole this time," Garmadon joked. Then they jumped, one at a time.

They landed in a room that looked like a cave, with rough ridges on the stone walls. Wu heard a tiny trickling sound and followed it to a small stream of water cascading down the rocks into a large, shallow stone. No torches lit the space, but glowing blue and green mushrooms sprouted from cracks in the rocky walls, giving the room an eerie light. Radiant white

reptiles, no bigger than Wu's hand, skittered around
the cave, adding to the brightness.

"Home, sweet home," Shezada said, and she
motioned to some small boulders. "Have a seat."

"So, you came here to this pyramid on purpose?"
Wu asked her.

"Sure," Shezada replied. "I came to get a wish
from the Sphinx, just like anyone else foolish enough
to come here."

"You said you've been here for weeks," Wu said, as
they all sat down. "Does that mean you haven't figured
out how to get out?"

"Not yet," she replied. "But I'm trying. Every day I
get a little closer."

"Have you met anyone else in here?" Garmadon asked.

Shezada's face clouded. "Well . . . not exactly. Not like you guys, anyway."

Wu was about to ask what she meant by that, but Garmadon interrupted with more questions.

"How have you managed to survive here for weeks? Is there a restaurant or something? Or a gift shop?" he asked.

"Well, I brought some supplies with me when I decided to enter the pyramid," Shezada replied. She nodded toward a small sack on a piece of rock that served as a table. "Mostly a bunch of sesame flour cookies. They're hard as rocks, but they don't go bad, and they fill you up."

Gurrrrrgle.

Garmadon's mostly-empty stomach rumbled at the mention of cookies. Shezada jumped up and aimed her spear in front of her.

"What was that?"

"Um, nothing," Garmadon said. "So is this, like, your home base?"

Shezada nodded and motioned around the cave. "I lucked out when I found this place. It might not look like much, but this fresh water is keeping me alive. And those brillies are filled with protein."

"Brillies?" Garmadon asked.

Shezada walked to the wall and quickly grabbed one of the glowing reptiles by the tail. "They're easy to catch, and they taste like chicken," she said. "Well, if the chicken lived in an algae-filled pool of muck."

She dropped the lizard, and it ran away. Then she nodded toward a stone bowl nestled in a pile of glowing embers. "I made a fresh pot of brillie stew this morning. Want some?"

"No thanks," both brothers answered at once.

"I mean, algae-filled muck chicken sounds tempting, but . . ." Wu began, and Shezada grinned.

"Wait until you've been here a few weeks," she said. "You'll change your tune."

"Oh, we do not plan on being here that long," Garmadon insisted.

"You think so, huh? That's cute," Shezada said. Then she shrugged. "Don't know what you're missing." As she bent down to spoon some stew into a bowl, Wu saw Garmadon reach into the sack and grab one of the cookies Shezada had talked about. He thought about calling out Garmadon, but who knew how Shezada would react? She seemed like a tough cookie herself. Hopefully she wouldn't notice one missing.

"So, you two must be here for a wish," she said. "What are you wishing for?"

"Why don't you tell us first?" Garmadon asked.

"Because I asked first," Shezada replied.

Wu looked at his brother, who shrugged.

"Well, our father sent us on this journey to find a special tea," Wu explained. "It only grows near the Northern Ocean."

Shezada raised an eyebrow. "Wow, that must be some tasty tea," she said. "The Northern Ocean is a long way off."

"Actually, it's supposed to have the ability to get rid of evil, or something like that," Wu explained, and Garmadon jabbed his brother with his elbow.

Shezada looked from Wu to Garmadon. "Which one of you is turning evil?"

Wu looked at the ceiling, and Garmadon looked at the floor. Shezada laughed. "That's okay. I'm sure I'll figure it out."

"All right, so what's your wish?" Wu asked.

Shezada's face clouded. "You know what? I should never have asked," she answered. Then she got up and rinsed her bowl in the trickling water. Wu saw Garmadon stealthily slip the stolen cookie back into the sack.

A brillie skittered across the wall, and Wu noticed something—chalk drawings on a smooth section. He walked over to the drawings. They looked like a giant map—a map of the maze.

"Shezada, what's all this?" he asked.

"Oh, yes! I was just about to show you that," she said and looked at the map. "You see, you need a strategy to get through this maze."

Wu glanced at Garmadon. "That's exactly what *I* said, dear brother, isn't it?"

Garmadon rolled his eyes.

"Every day I leave this room for hours and explore the maze," she explained. "I go a little farther each day, and when I get back, I create a map so I won't take the same path twice."

Wu nodded. "That's really smart."

She grinned. "Thanks! I think I'm finally close to finding my way out. I've survived every challenge the maze has thrown at me, and I'm pretty sure I can handle any other surprises this pyramid is holding."

Garmadon marched up to them. "Wait a second, you said you've been in here for *weeks*?" he asked. "So how much longer do you think you will need to get out?"

Shezada shrugged. "If my hunch is right, not much longer. But it could take a few more weeks. I just don't know."

"Great. We'll probably *never* get out of here," Garmadon mumbled.

"You're right," Shezada agreed. "You don't have what it takes to get out of here alive!"

Chapter 6
The Smart-Mouthed Sphinx

"You really think we don't have what it takes to get out of here alive?" Garmadon asked Shezada. "We're not your average adventurers. We're the sons of the First Spinjitzu Master!"

Shezada carefully eyed them both. "That's very interesting," she said. "Because I'm pretty sure I could have defeated you both back there if our fight had continued."

Something in the girl's voice made Garmadon believe her. He raised an eyebrow. "I guess we'll never know."

"I think we'll surprise you when you see all of our skills," Wu added.

She frowned. "I normally don't like surprises. Surprises can throw you off your game. But I guess there's strength in numbers. I'm warning you, though—if you hold me back, you're on your own."

Garmadon watched her carefully. *I feel like we can trust her,* he thought. *But there's definitely more to her than what we see. She's clearly a skilled fighter, and smart, too. But she hasn't told us anything about herself.*

"You know who we are," Garmadon said. "So what's your story?"

Shezada yawned. "It's time to rest. If we're going to try to get through the maze tomorrow, we should all get some sleep. Help yourself to some stew if you change your mind."

Then her eyes twinkled. "And this is for you, Garmadon. You just had to ask." She tossed him a sesame cookie.

Garmadon looked down and blushed a little. "Thanks," he said.

Shezada retreated to a secluded area of the cave. Garmadon and Wu spread out their bed rolls on the hard floor.

"I think we can trust her," Wu said, echoing his brother's thoughts.

"Yeah," Garmadon agreed. "Let's just hope she knows the way out. I don't want to spend any more time in this place than we have to."

Wu held out his hand. "You want to share that cookie?"

Garmadon hesitated, then broke the cookie and handed half of it to Wu. It was hard and crunchy, and it felt like a brick in his stomach, but Shezada was right—it filled him up.

The boys drifted off to sleep. In his dreams, Garmadon was falling . . . and falling . . . and falling . . . but never seemed to land. It was a relief when the sound of voices woke him up. Wu and Shezada were standing over a flat stone that acted as a table, talking excitedly.

"What's going on?" Garmadon asked, yawning.

"Your brother's a genius, that's what!" Shezada exclaimed. "He had some paper in his bag and he's been up for an hour, copying what I have on the wall. Now we have a map of the maze we can take with us. I didn't have anything to make a map out of, so I've just been using my memory, and I can't always remember every little twist and turn. This could really help. Good thinking, Wu."

Wu blushed. "It's no big deal. I'm just lucky I had some paper with me. I was going to keep a journal of this trip, but there hasn't been any time to write."

Garmadon watched them. Shezada was, well . . . really cool and funny, and had maybe the most beautiful eyes he'd ever seen. And there she was with Wu, talking and laughing. Of course she was talking with his practically perfect, not-potentially-evil brother, and not him. He felt a twinge. Was it jealousy?

I'm not jealous, he told himself. *So what if she likes Wu better than she likes me?* But the feeling didn't go away.

"All right, then," Shezada said. She slung her bag over her shoulder, along with an archer's bow. "Our goal is to reach the Sphinx's chamber."

Garmadon and Wu strapped on their packs.

"What do we need to watch out for?" Wu asked.

"I can get us through the first few challenges," Shezada replied. "Just follow me, and do what I do."

Garmadon headed for an opening in the cave wall. "Is this the way out?"

"Yes, but—"

wHooSH!

A stream of fire shot at Garmadon as he stepped through the opening. The ninja quickly jumped back.

"What the—?" Against the wall in front of him was a small statue of the Sphinx, no taller than Garmadon. The statue's eyes were glowing red jewels.

"Good morning, Garmadon!" the statue purred evilly, in the Sphinx's voice. "Ready for Shezada to lead you to your doom?"

Shezada came up behind him. "Ignore her," she told him. "These statues are all over the maze, and it's how the Sphinx communicates. She tries to get under your skin."

"Shezada is *so good* at failing," the statue taunted.

"You're looking extra evil today, Sphinx," Shezada said cheerfully. "Come on, guys."

They followed her down a corridor, away from the statue. As they walked, she took a better grip on her spear.

"Danger ahead?" Wu asked.

"Always," Shezada replied. "But coming up is what I like to call Scorpion Highway."

"Scorpions? As in creepy bugs with sharp pincers and spear-like tails?" Garmadon remarked.

"Yup. Giant ones," she replied. "And thanks to the Sphinx, they're indestructible. Their only weakness is a small, blue spot on their bellies. Hit that and they go numb for a few minutes."

"That's convenient," Wu said.

Shezada shook her head. "Flipping giant scorpions is not as easy as it sounds."

They had reached the end of the corridor. Shezada took a deep breath.

"Good luck!" she said, and then she turned the corner. "When you reach the end, turn left!"

Garmadon grinned at Wu. "Once again, the left turn is the right choice!"

They turned left. A sea of scorpions headed toward them, legs clacking on the stone floor. Each one was the size of a farmyard pig, with two claws that had sharp pincers, eight legs, a curved, poisonous tail, and a shiny blue exoskeleton. Dozens of beady black eyes gleamed in the torchlight.

Shezada charged forward, thrusting her spear at the first scorpion in her path. The creature landed on its back, and she pressed the blunt end of her spear into its belly. Its tail and legs stopped flailing.

"Nice trick!" Garmadon complimented her.

"Yeah, well, I could use some help!" she shot back.

Garmadon and Wu came up behind her, using their fighting staffs to bash the scorpions as they plowed through the creatures. The sharp brush of claws against Garmadon's leg caused his adrenaline to surge, and he used the staff to pick up each scorpion in his path from underneath, sending them flying.

"Ninjaaagoooooo!" Wu cried, and he whirled past Shezada. The wind from his tornado flipped the scorpions onto their backs, and Shezada struck each one in its weak spot, numbing it.

With Shezada and Wu working together, the three of them reached the end of the corridor and turned left. Garmadon leaned back against the wall, breathing heavily.

"We did it!" Wu cheered.

"Yeah, thanks for the assist, Whirlwind," Shezada told Wu, and she smiled.

Garmadon felt that pang again. *Why don't I get a nickname?*

"The next challenge isn't far," Shezada said. "Just a couple of turns."

Wu took the map from his pocket. "Yeah, a right turn and then a left."

They all walked forward.

"So, did your father teach you those moves, Whirlwind?" Shezada asked.

"Yes," Wu replied. "I've been studying Spinjitzu ever since I can remember."

I've been studying? Garmadon thought. *Don't you mean we, brother?*

Annoyed by the conversation, Garmadon jogged ahead of Wu and Shezada. He made a left turn into a dark passageway.

It's not fair! Didn't Shezada see me send those scorpions flying? he wondered, as he stomped through the maze. *Not every situation calls for a Spinjitzu tornado. Wu was just showing off. . . .*

He came to a crossroads and remembered Wu's words. Right and then a left. He made a left turn . . .

. . . and dropped into another void!

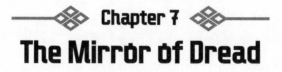

Chapter 7
The Mirror of Dread

Before Garmadon could brace himself for another fall, he felt a hand grip his arm and pull him back. He turned, expecting to see Wu, but it was Shezada who had saved him.

"You're welcome," she said with a grin.

"Thanks," Garmadon said. "Wu said to turn left. . . ."

"Yeah, but there's a drop as soon as you make the turn," Shezada said. "Another one of the Sphinx's tricks. It's easy enough to jump over, though, if you care to look."

Garmadon saw that the drop he had fallen through wasn't wide at all. Shezada leapt over it to the other side, and the brothers did the same.

"Listen up! I know you two are big time ninja and everything, but you might want to stick with me from now on," Shezada said. "I know this part of the maze really well."

"You don't have to convince *me*," Wu said, and Garmadon rolled his eyes.

"I just got a few steps ahead of you both," he said defensively. "You could have warned me."

"Sorry about that, brother," Wu said. "You ran ahead before I could say anything more."

"Hmph." *What kind of apology was that?* Garmadon wondered.

They reached another turn in the maze. A small Sphinx statue sat there.

"Lost your footing, Garmadon?" the statue asked. "Was that some secret Spinjitzu move your father taught you?"

"Very funny," Garmadon grumbled.

"Actually, I'm glad you made it this far," the statue continued. "I think you'll like this next section. Have fun, but don't get stung!"

"Have fun? Is this a circus or a deadly maze?" Wu asked. He turned to Shezada. "What does she mean by 'don't get stung'?"

Shezada nodded toward the turn. "I call this one the Pokey Passage," she answered. "Spears come in and out of the wall at random, and you have to be quick to get through them without being struck. I'll go through first; you follow my lead."

The three of them turned the corner.

"Good luck! You're going to need it!" the statue called out.

The passage ahead was empty, but Garmadon did notice dozens of holes in the walls on either side. Shezada took a deep breath.

"Here goes."

She stepped forward, and the spears began to pop in and out of the walls randomly. One would retract, and another one would pop out in a different place.

Shezada moved quickly, jumping, somersaulting, and even crawling to avoid the spears. After a few tense minutes, she reached the end of the corridor.

"I'll go next!" Garmadon announced.

"Trying to impress Shezada?" Wu asked in a low voice behind him.

"I don't need to impress anybody," Garmadon replied, but he had to admit his brother was right. The other reason he wanted to go first was because he was nervous and wanted to get it over with.

Focus, G, he told himself. He took a deep breath and he stepped into the corridor. The spears began to shoot out.

Ziiiip! A spear popped out low from the right wall, and Garmadon jumped over it.

Ziiiip! One from the left nearly grazed his head, and he ducked. Garmadon realized he had to split his focus between both walls.

Ziiiip! Another one from the left shot out at waist height, and he somersaulted over it, as he had seen Shezada do.

"Almost halfway through, Garmadon!" Shezada called out. "You're doing great!"

The encouragement gave him a burst of energy. He ducked, dove, and jumped through the corridor until he reached her. She grinned at him.

"Great job!"

Wu was already halfway through the course. He finished swiftly and landed with a leap next to Shezada.

"Looks like we all made it," he said, and Shezada high-fived him. Then her eyes got wide.

"Hey, Whirlwind, what's that?" She pointed to a scratch on his neck.

"Oh, one of the arrows nicked me, but it's no big deal," he replied.

Shezada shook her head. "It's *kind of* a big deal. I didn't want to make you nervous, so I didn't tell you earlier, but there's poison on the spear tips. My first time through, I met a guy who'd been stuck by a spear."

"What happened to him?" Wu asked.

Shezada bit her lip. "The poison spread through his body pretty quickly, and . . ."

Garmadon's stomach dropped. "You mean, Wu . . ."

Shezada nodded. "He doesn't have long."

Wu's face froze, and Garmadon saw real fear in his brother's eyes. Garmadon turned to Shezada.

"There's got to be something we can do!" he cried.

Red light lit up the passageway, revealing another Sphinx statue.

"Your friend is a goner," the statue said. "But I'm not a *total* monster. The venom of the green spider is the cure."

Then the statue's eyes went dark.

"Green spiders?" Garmadon asked.

"I know where to find them, but we have to get there quickly," Shezada replied. "We'll take a detour."

"You're not going to ditch us?" Wu asked in a frightened voice.

"Ah, it's just a small detour," she mumbled. "Come on, let's go."

Garmadon glanced at his brother. Wu looked pale and worried. Garmadon also noticed that the scratch on his neck was starting to bubble and turn black.

"You're going to be fine," Garmadon assured him, but his brother didn't reply.

They followed Shezada through the maze. They swung on ropes across a lava pit and leapt over a river of hissing snakes. Then they reached a cliff with a huge drop below. A narrow rock ridge jutted out of the cliff, and it was the only way to keep going and maybe finding some way to get around the looming abyss.

"This doesn't look too hard," Wu said hopefully. "It just takes balance, right?"

Shezada turned to face them both. "It's trickier than that," she replied. "The path takes you past what I like to call the Mirror of Dread. Whatever you do, don't look into it!"

"Why not?" Garmadon asked.

A dark look crossed Shezada's face. "I looked into it the first time I passed through here. What I saw freaked me out so much that I almost fell into the abyss."

"What did you see?" Garmadon pressed her.

Shezada turned away. "Just some bad memories."

Garmadon and Wu exchanged glances.

Shezada sure likes to keep secrets, Garmadon thought.

She turned back to them. "Listen, I don't have time to explain it to you right now. It's . . . Just don't look in the mirror, okay?"

They slowly inched their way along the ridge, which wasn't much wider than their feet. Garmadon pressed his body against the cliff wall.

"It gets wider up ahead," Shezada promised. "That's where the mirror is. When you get there, close your eyes and take five steps. Then open them again."

Garmadon watched Shezada and then Wu walk past the mirror. When it was his turn, Garmadon closed his eyes. He took one step, then two . . .

Just one quick look won't hurt, a little voice inside him said. *What could have possibly scared Shezada so much? Bad memories? I'm not afraid of my past. And I bet she'd be impressed if I looked into the mirror without freaking out. . . .*

He opened his eyes. His reflection stared back at him from a large mirror with an ornate frame.

What's the big deal? he wondered, but then the reflection changed. . . .

His reflection grew taller, older—and then he changed completely into something not quite human. Pure white hair topped a face as black and cold as midnight in winter. His eyes had become two red glowing orbs. Instead of two arms, he had four—and two of his hands held swords.

There were two figures in silhouette next to the terrifying figure, with their backs turned to him. One looked like a kid. Garmadon stared, transfixed.

Is that future guy . . . me? Is my father right? Is there really evil inside me? And those people—why are they turned away from me?

A feeling of utter loneliness and despair swept over him. He couldn't take his eyes off the image.

"Noooooooooo!" he wailed.

Chapter 8
Just a Little Bite

In the mirror, Garmadon watched as some invisible force suddenly pulled him back. He blinked as he realized that Shezada had rescued him.

"I told you not to look!" she scolded him. "Are you okay?"

"I'm fine," Garmadon answered, but it was a lie. That terrible, lonely feeling still lingered.

Shezada looked straight into his eyes for a while and nodded. Garmadon was grateful she wasn't giving him more of a hard time.

"Come on," she said. "We're close to the spiders."

They traveled down another corridor that took them past a small cave. Inside, silvery webs hung from the ceiling, each one containing a glittering green spider.

Wu approached one of the webs. "How is this supposed to cure me?" He shuddered. "I'm not supposed to eat one, am I?"

A red glow came from the corner of the cave. It was another Sphinx statue.

"Had a little scare there, Garmadon?" the statue taunted.

Garmadon scowled. "I made it here, didn't I? Now, how are these spiders supposed to help my brother?"

"Just one little bite, and he'll be all right!" the statue rhymed.

Wu turned pale. "So I *do* have to eat it?"

"No!" the Sphinx yelled. "The spider needs to give *you* one little bite."

Wu frowned. "I'm not sure that's much better."

Garmadon got a closer look at one of the spiders. It had two teeny, but very sharp-looking fangs.

Wu looked at Shezada. "Do you think this is a trick of the Sphinx?" he asked. "What if the bite has . . . side effects?"

Side effects . . . he's thinking of when I got bitten by the Great Devourer, Garmadon thought.

"Don't worry, Wu. When we have the tea, I'll share it with you," he joked.

Shezada raised an eyebrow at Garmadon. "So *you're* the evil one? Yeah, that makes sense."

"What do you mean?" Garmadon asked, but she didn't reply.

"I think you should let the spider bite you," she told his brother. "The Sphinx is cruel but fair. I believe it's the only way to save you."

Wu gritted his teeth, closed his eyes, and placed his hand on one of the webs. A spider crawled over to him and sank its fangs into Wu's hand.

Wu yelped, and the spider retreated back to the top of the web. Wu let out a long breath.

"How will I know if it's working?" he asked.

"Well, we can keep an eye on that gnarly neck of yours," Shezada said. "I didn't want to say anything, but it got pretty nasty looking on the way over here."

Garmadon nodded. "Yeah, I noticed it, too. Kinda black and bubbling."

"Seriously?" Wu asked, feeling his neck. "What about now?"

A blue glow rose on Wu's neck. The angry, bubbling scratch faded, leaving nothing but smooth skin.

"It worked!" Garmadon cried, and he was surprised at how relieved he felt. It would have been awful if something bad had happened to his brother. "You look good to me, Wu."

"Yeah, you look great," Shezada said. "And now we can keep moving. Whirlwind, can you look at the map? What's the best way to get back over to the end of the Pokey Passage?"

Wu looked at the map. "Here's a way with some twists and turns, but it's shorter than going back past the Mirror of Dread."

"Lead the way, then," Shezada said, and Wu grinned at her.

Garmadon looked at the stone Sphinx. "Thanks for telling us how to save my brother."

"Oh, don't thank me!" the statue replied. "I just saved him so I could see something more exciting defeat him than a wall of spears. You three are awfully entertaining."

Garmadon scowled, and the three of them left the spider cave. Wu led them down a series of dark, narrow corridors with what seemed like endless twists and turns.

Garmadon moved next to Shezada.

"You know," he began, "you seem to know a lot about us. Who we are, what our wish is. But we don't know anything about you."

Shezada turned her head, and her dark eyes locked on his.

"That's fair," she said. "I'm from the village of Haru—have you heard of it?"

Garmadon shook his head. "I don't think so."

"That's because a flash flood wiped it out years ago—when I was a kid," she replied. "Almost everything—and everyone—was wiped out."

Her eyes look haunted, Garmadon thought. *I wonder who she lost?*

"I've been on my own since then," Shezada continued. "Searching for treasure, trying to rebuild the village."

Garmadon nodded. "Is that what your wish is for? Treasure?"

Shezada looked away. "My wish will be that the flood never happened."

Just like I want to wish that I never got bitten, Garmadon mused. *But can a wish really do that? What would my life be like if I'd never been bitten that day?*

"Hey, you two, hold up!" Wu called behind him. "There's something up here on the map, Shezada, you call it the Quicksand Trap."

She nodded. "Oh, that's right! I discovered this a few weeks ago. Let's get a closer look, and I'll explain."

The hall opened onto a platform, and beyond that, a series of round stone posts stretched to a platform on the other side. The posts rose from what looked like wet sand.

"That's quicksand," Shezada explained. "Some of the posts are steady. Others sink into the quicksand when you stop on them. They sink pretty quickly, so it's best to avoid them. Luckily, I remembered the sequence. Two, three, one, four, two, one, three."

"Two, three, one, four, two, one, three," the brothers repeated.

Wu looked at Garmadon. "Don't go rogue this time, brother."

Garmadon frowned. "Yeah? Well, how about you don't get poisoned."

"How about you two stop bickering and focus?" Shezada asked, and she jumped onto the second post. She jumped over the next two and landed on the third one in front of her. Then she jumped to the very next post.

"Two, three, one," she said. "Come on, let's stick together."

Wu went next, jumping to the second post, then jumping three ahead. Garmadon jumped to the second post next.

"This the hardest one," Shezada said. "Gotta jump over three posts and land on the fourth."

She launched off the column, leapt over the next three, and landed on the fourth with perfect balance.

Then the column began to quickly sink underneath her feet!

"No way, I—I know it was four!" she yelled, and she jumped onto the next post. That one started to sink, too.

"The Sphinx must have changed the sequence!" she yelled. As she spoke, all the posts began to sink into the quicksand.

"Hurry!" Shezada yelled. "We've got to get to the other side!"

But Wu didn't move.

"Wait!" he cried. "Look up!"

Garmadon gazed upward to see a hole in the ceiling, with a ladder coming down from it. "Another way out? Should we take it?"

"It could be the way to the Sphinx's chamber!" Wu sounded excited.

Shezada hesitated. "You could be right, Wu."

The quicksand was already lapping at their feet.

"I'm checking it out!" Wu cried, and he leapt, grabbed the bottom rung of the ladder, and pulled himself up.

"I don't see any other choice," Shezada said, and she quickly jumped back toward Garmadon. Then she leapt up and joined Wu. Garmadon did the same.

He climbed the ladder and joined the others in a dark passageway.

"I've definitely never been here before," Shezada remarked. "Let's move forward carefully."

They walked down the passage and through an open doorway. A Sphinx statue sat in the middle of the room. It's red eyes glowed.

"I've got some good news and some bad news," the statue said. "The good news is, you've made it! You're one step away from the Sphinx's chamber."

"What's the bad news, then?" Garmadon asked.

The statue cackled. "Nobody ever gets out of this room alive!"

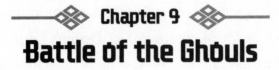

Chapter 9
Battle of the Ghouls

Slam! The door shut behind them. All three quickly scanned the room. On either wall was a round entrance leading into a dark tunnel.

"I see two ways out," Garmadon said.

The Sphinx statue's eyes flashed as she laughed. "Why don't you pick one? Although, whichever way you pick, it will probably lead to disaster and doom."

Garmadon, Wu, and Shezada approached the tunnel on the right. A loud groaning sound came from the darkness.

"I think something's in there," Wu said anxiously. He looked at the other tunnel. "The same sound is coming from there, too."

"We need to stick together," Shezada said. "Center of the room, with our backs to each other. We'll be ready for whatever's in there."

They got into position, but they weren't ready for the creatures that poured out of the tunnels. Green ghouls with blank eyes stumbled into the room, drool dripping from their mouths. Dozens and dozens poured in like a wave of the undead. Moaning and groaning, they reached for the three living beings in the room.

"Gross!" Garmadon yelled, holding his fighting staff in front of him defensively. "You mean we've got to get through these moldy monsters to get to the Sphinx?"

The crowds of ghouls were almost pressing in on them now.

"There's too many!" Shezada yelled. "We need a strategy."

"Normally I'd agree, but I don't think we have time for a strategy," Wu said, and he charged at the ghouls descending on him, striking the nearest with his staff. The ghoul flew across the room, and Wu moved on to the next.

"Good work, brother!" Garmadon called.

Bam!

He struck the ghoul closest to him, sending him thudding to the ground.

"Whack-a-ghoul!" he cried out, and he began pummeling ghouls, one by one.

Nearby, Shezada sent her arrows whizzing at the ghouls, but it didn't stop them. It only slowed them down. With an eerie growl, one of them tore the bow out of her hands.

"They may drool like babies, but they're strong!" she called, and she jumped, landing with each foot

on top of a ghoul's shoulder. Then she jumped and landed on another one.

"If you can't beat them, jump on them!" she joked as she made her way across the crowd of ghouls toward the tunnel.

"Right behind you!" Garmadon replied.

Bam! Bam!

He sent another ghoul to his knees, and then another. But it wasn't easy. More and more ghouls descended on him. One grabbed Garmadon's arm, sending a strange chill through his whole body.

"Enough of this!" Garmadon cried, freeing his arm. *"Ninjaaaaaaaago!"*

Garmadon spun into a Spinjitzu tornado, barreling through the crowd of ghouls at top speed. He reached the tunnel and found Shezada inside.

"We did it!" he cried, and they high-fived.

"Wait," Shezada said. "Where's Wu?"

Garmadon spun around. The ghouls were behind them—and so was Wu, unless he'd somehow escaped through the other tunnel.

"He'll be fine," Garmadon said quickly. "We should keep moving, Shezada. Wu's got the map, he's strong, and he'll find us. We need to get out of here while we can, before the ghouls figure out where we are."

A dark thought popped into his mind. *If Wu doesn't find us, would that be so bad? I wouldn't have to listen to him and Father anymore. I could end this dumb search for a tea that probably wouldn't work anyway. I could even hang with Shezada and go treasure hunting if I wanted to. . . .*

Shezada's voice interrupted his thoughts. "Are you sure you just want to keep going?" she asked. "I mean, I'm all for self-preservation, but he *is* your brother."

The image from the Mirror of Dread suddenly struck him like a fighting staff. That image of his future, evil self. That feeling of unbearable loneliness as those two figures turned away from him. He never wanted to feel like that—ever. And somehow, he knew that abandoning Wu now was the first step toward becoming that person.

He nodded. "All right. Let's go back in there."

Shezada grinned. "I'll jump, you spin."

"I'll smash," he said, holding up his sword. "It'll be easier to find Wu if I'm not moving at whirlwind speed."

They both charged back into the chamber. A hollow-eyed ghoul immediately lunged for Garmadon.

Bam!

Garmadon whacked him aside. Two more ghouls converged on them, and Garmadon swiftly dispatched them.

Bam! Bam!

"Over here!" Shezada called out, and he followed the sound of her voice, keeping another ghoul at bay with a roundhouse kick.

Shezada had ridden the shoulders of ghouls to the other entrance to the chamber. She'd run out of ghouls to jump on because the floor here was littered with groaning ghoul bodies.

"Wu must have gotten out this way," she said. "Come on."

Garmadon followed her into the tunnel.

"Ow!" Shezada cried. A stray ghoul had lunged at her, and she pushed him away. He landed at Garmadon's feet. Garmadon jumped over him.

"Did that thing hurt you?" he asked Shezada.

"It's nothing," she replied. "Let's go find Wu."

They raced down the corridor, made a few turns, and finally came to Wu, standing in front of another Sphinx statue.

"Whirlwind!" Shezada cried.

"I knew you'd find me!" he said. He held out the map. "Your map doesn't go this far, but I've been thinking. We must be close to the chamber. And since

we fell through a trap door that put us down here, the chamber must be above us."

Wu looked up and frowned. "The only thing is, I don't see a way up."

Shezada looked thoughtful. "There's probably a trick to it. There always is, in this place."

The statue's eyes lit up. "No trick!" the Sphinx said. "Just keep your balance!"

"Balance?" Garmadon echoed, and then the floor underneath the three of them began to shake. A round stone pillar pushed up, with them standing on top. The pillar slowly began to rise.

Garmadon looked up. A round stone in the ceiling slid to the side, creating an opening for the pillar.

"That must be the chamber up there!" Shezada cried. "I have a good feeling about this!"

"What if it's a trick?" Wu asked.

It better not be a trick, Garmadon thought. *I want my wish. I want to wish that snake had never bitten me so there's no chance of me becoming a lonely, evil monster!*

Chapter 10
The Blue Warriors

"For once we're going up and not tumbling down into an abyss," Wu joked as they rose up toward the ceiling.

"Yeah, that tricky Sphinx sure loves trap doors," Garmadon agreed.

Wu grinned at his brother. *I hope the Sphinx isn't messing with us,* he thought. *I want Garmadon to get his wish. And maybe I'll wish for . . . I'm not sure? Father's approval? Is that even something you can wish for?*

The pillar reached the opening in the ceiling, and when it ground to a stop, Wu saw that they indeed were in a chamber—but it wasn't the chamber of the Sphinx. Instead, twelve fearsome warriors guarded a tall arched doorway.

Wu quickly held his staff in a defensive position, sizing up the warriors as Garmadon and Shezada did the same. Sharp pincers extended from the mouth of each glowing-eyed warrior. They wore identical armor made of shiny blue metal, and their helmets reminded Wu of an insect, with two short black antennae protruding from each one. They carried blunt weapons with a blade shaped like a jagged bug leg on each end.

"No one shall enter the Chamber of the Sphinx without going through *us*," the warriors said in unison, in strange, buzzy voices.

Garmadon sighed. "Will this ever end?"

"It's just one more challenge," Shezada said. "I've been stuck in this place for too long. Let's do this."

She held her spear with both hands, pointing it forward. "CHAAAAAAARGE!" She raced toward the warriors.

Oddly, the warriors didn't move. They stayed in position, waiting. Shezada jumped and thrust her spear through the metal armor of one of the warrior's before her feet touched the floor again.

"This is too easy!" she cried, but then the warriors' body began to tremble and a chattering, clattering sound rose from it. Suddenly the body transformed into thousands of blue scarabs! They swarmed around Shezada, racing up her body, approaching her neck. . . .

"*Ninjaaaaaaago!*" Wu yelled, and he whirled toward Shezada in a Spinjitzu tornado. As he whirled, he grabbed her hand. Then he pulled her into the tornado with him, sending the beetles flying off her.

Some of the beetles landed on Garmadon. "Watch it!" he yelled, batting them off, and squashing some under his feet with a loud crunch.

Wu and Shezada came to a stop.

"Thanks, Whirlwind" she said. "How do you do that without getting dizzy?"

Wu grinned. "I still *do* get dizzy," he told her.

The warriors marched toward them now.

"Try to get to the door without hitting any of them!" Garmadon called, but he quickly realized that

would be impossible. Two of the warriors charged at him with blades drawn, and Garmadon whacked them away with his staff. Both warriors dissolved into beetles, covering Garmadon in an instant. He spun through the mass of insects, but many still clung to him, nipping him with their sharp mouth pincers.

Wu and Shezada worked in sync. Each time the girl stabbed a warrior, Wu took her hand and spun to shake off the beetles.

Four . . . five . . . six . . . Garmadon and Shezada attacked the warriors one by one. By the time they reached the last warrior—and the door—the room was filled with beetles. The three could barely move.

"I see the door!" Garmadon cried.

Wu pushed a beetle away from his mouth. "Yes! All three of us together—push!"

They pushed with all of their might, and the heavy door opened. A bright light shone through, and the beetles scattered and withdrew.

Together, they stepped in the Sphinx's chamber. She sat there, as enormous as before, with a grin on her face.

"We did it!" Wu cheered.

"Happy to see us?" Garmadon asked the Sphinx.

"No," the Sphinx replied. "I'm smiling because your happiness will soon be dashed."

"What do you mean?" Garmadon asked.

Wu heard a groan and turned to Shezada. Her skin had turned a sickly gray, and both of her eyes were pure black!

"Did the beetles do this?" he asked.

The Sphinx cackled. "No," she answered. "Your friend is turning into a ghoul!"

Chapter 11
One Wish

Garmadon looked at Shezada. "Back there, when we went to find Wu . . ."

She nodded. "That ghoul that surprised me bit me."

"No one has gotten past the ghouls without getting bitten," the Sphinx said. "And those who get bitten become ghouls themselves. That's why I have so many ghouls. It's a great system, actually."

Garmadon's stomach tightened. He'd wanted to leave Wu behind. Shezada had convinced him to go back, and now she was the one suffering. . . .

Wu stepped forward. "Our wishes!" he cried. "Shezada, use your wish to get better."

"Think carefully," the Sphinx said. "The three of you entered the chamber together, so you only get one wish."

Garmadon's eyes flashed with anger. Wu's face turned pale. Shezada's shoulders slumped.

"That's not fair!" Wu cried. "You never said that!"

"My pyramid, my rules," the Sphinx replied. "I make them up as I go."

Wu clenched his fists. He looked at his brother. "We could battle her," he said in desperation. "*Make* her give Shezada her wish."

Garmadon shook his head. "It won't work, Wu. I know how the Sphinx's mind works. You can't force her to do something just by fighting with her. Maybe if we negotiate."

"This is not up for negotiation!" the Sphinx snapped. "You'd better decide quickly. You three have one wish. Will you use it to help the girl?"

"Wait!" Wu cried. "Couldn't we do a wish to help them both? A wish that both Garmadon and Shezada are healed?"

"One got bitten by a snake, the other got bitten by a ghoul," the Sphinx replied. "That's still two wishes in my book. Now, DECIDE!"

The vision from the mirror flashed in Garmadon's head once more, and now he felt a feeling of despair. Somehow, he felt in his bones that he could not escape his destiny.

But he *could* help Shezada.

"I say yes," Garmadon said.

Wu looked at his brother. "That wish could save you, brother. Are you sure?"

"We have to help Shezada," Garmadon replied. "Besides, I keep telling you, I don't need saving."

Wu nodded. "It's the only thing to do."

Shezada said nothing. She stared blankly forward with hollow eyes.

"Heal her!" Garmadon cried. "Back to the way she was before she got bitten by the ghoul."

The Sphinx raised her eyebrows. "As you wish," she said, and her eyes sparkled. Between Wu and Garmadon, Shezada glowed with white light. When the light disappeared, she looked completely normal.

She blinked. "What . . . what happened?" she asked.

"The Sphinx gave us one wish, and we used it so you wouldn't turn into a ghoul," Wu replied.

For once, Garmadon didn't mind Wu speaking for both of them. *I did the right thing,* he told himself. *That's all that matters.*

Shezada's eyes widened. "But I—"

The door to the pyramid slid open. "Please leave me now," the Sphinx said. "Unless you'd like to remain here in the pyramid?"

"No, we're good!" Garmadon said. He grabbed Shezada by the hand and pulled her toward the door. Wu followed.

They left the pyramid, and the door slammed shut behind them. Some of the pyramid-hatted villagers noticed and stared at them in wonder.

Shezada turned to Garmadon. "Let me get this straight. The Sphinx only gave us one wish, and instead of using it to fix yourself, you saved me."

Garmadon shrugged. "It was an easy choice."

"Thanks, Garmadon," she said, and she kissed him on the cheek. He blushed. "You know, for a supposedly evil guy, you're really a softie. Maybe that's what I'll call you. Softie."

Garmadon shook his head. "Can't I get a cool nickname, like Whirlwind?"

Wu laughed. "I think it's perfect, Softie."

Garmadon shook his head. "You know, Shezada, I was going to ask you to come on our journey with us, but now . . ." he teased.

"I'd turn you down anyway," she said. "I may not be able to change the past, but I can keep helping people who need help right now. I've got a lead on some treasure."

"Aw, come on, Shezada, you can always search for treasure," Garmadon said. "Just take a little detour with us. What do you say?"

"We all worked great together in the pyramid," Wu said. "Isn't it better to be on a team than to be alone?"

Before Shezada could answer, a crowd of villagers swarmed them, asking questions.

"They survived the pyramid!"

"What did you wish for?"

"How did you survive the Sphinx?"

Garmadon and Wu pushed through them as politely as they could. Then Garmadon saw a masked figure slipping away.

"Shezada!" he called, but the treasure hunter disappeared in the crowd.

Neither boy spoke for a minute.

"She was really awesome," Wu finally said.

"Yeah," Garmadon agreed. *And beautiful. And smart. And mysterious . . .* He sighed. "What now?"

Wu looked around. "Maybe we can get some food and find a place to rest?" he asked. "Then we can figure out the quickest way to get to the Northern Ocean."

"I say we follow the stars and forget about any shortcuts," Garmadon replied. "Look where the last one got us!"

"Well, we wouldn't have met Shezada," Wu said, and the two boys were quiet once more.

Then Wu spoke up again. "You know, I'm glad we ended up in that pyramid. Because I learned something important. It's that I can always count on you, brother." He patted Garmadon's shoulder. "You thought I was lost, and you came to find me. You *are* a softie."

Garmadon looked away from Wu, remembering how close he had come to leaving his brother in the pyramid. For a second, he thought about confessing what had happened, but then he quickly changed his mind. "I think I smell meat cooking over there," he said. "Let's check it out."

Maybe I do *need that tea,* Garmadon thought as they walked across the sand together. *I just hope . . . I hope that when we find it, it's not too late.*

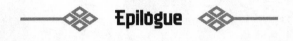

Epilogue

"Did you ever see Shezada again, Whirlwind?" Jay teased Master Wu.

Master Wu and the ninja had reached the barbecue restaurant and were seated around a table with a hot griddle in the center. A white-coated chef used two spatulas to quickly stir-fry meat and vegetables. The food smelled great, but the ninja still gazed at Wu.

A faraway look appeared in Master Wu's eyes, and he didn't answer right away.

"I did see Shezada again," he finally replied, "but that is a story for another time."

"Well, I hope you tell us about it one day," Nya said. "Shezada seems supercool. And I kind of got

the impression that you and your brother both had a crush on her."

"Shezada was indeed quite remarkable," Master Wu said, and he quickly changed the subject. "Now, let us eat!"

Jay looked around. "Where's Kai?"

"In the restroom, trying to fix his hair," Nya answered. "Honestly, if he spent as much time on his Spinjitzu as he did on his hair, he would be—"

Kai walked up, on his way back from the restroom. "Luckily I keep emergency hair products with me at all times," he said, smoothing back his brown hair with one hand. "It's not perfect, but—"

wHoosH!

A giant flame rose from the hot grill.

"On it!" Nya cried, jumping up. She pushed forward with both hands and doused the flame with water— along with her brother, Kai.

"Whoops! Sorry, Kai," Nya said.

Kai sighed and sat down. "It's okay," he said.

"I guess I'm destined to have a bad hair day."

"A bad hair day, but a good time," Cole remarked, and the ninja dug into their meal.

Glossary

Cole

Cole is the Earth Ninja who wields the elemental power of Earth and supports his ninja friends with his confidence and great physical strength.

Beetle Warriors

These armored warriors have sharp pincers and glowing eyes. When attacked, they transform into thousands of blue scarab beetles.

Explorers' Club

This members-only club is for Ninjago world's most renowned explorers and archaeologists. It is managed by Cecil Putnam, who seems to care more about the club itself than about its members.

First Spinjitzu Master

This is the creator of Spinjitzu and the entire Ninjago world. He was also the father of Garmadon and Wu, whom he trained in the art of Spinjitzu to protect the world he had created.

Garmadon

A son of the First Spinjitzu Master, Garmadon grew up learning the ways of Spinjitzu with his brother, Wu. Bitten by a vile snake as a child, Garmadon gradually filled with evil to become Lord Garmadon, the greatest villain in the world of Ninjago.

Ghoul

Loud, slow, and smelly, but extremely dangerous, a ghoul preys on other living creatures. A person bitten by a ghoul from the Sphinx's pyramid turns into a ghoul themselves.

Great Devourer

This is the snake that bit Garmadon as a child and infected him with evil from its venom. After many years, the snake grew up to become a huge monster that almost destroyed Ninjago City.

Jay

The Lightning Ninja is quick-witted, talks fast, and often acts before he thinks. Jay also loves pranks and jokes. Without Jay's sense of humor, the ninja team would be in a much worse mood.

Kai

Nya's older brother is the Fire Ninja. With his fierce temper, bravery, and strong sense of justice, he'll stop at nothing if he has put his mind to it. This includes fixing his hair.

Lloyd

Wise beyond his years, Lloyd is the leader of the ninja team. He is the son of Garmadon and Misako. Lloyd once sought to follow in his father's evil footsteps, but with the help of the ninja, he fulfilled his destiny to become the Green Ninja.

Nya

Kai's younger sister is the Water Ninja. She's a skilled warrior, inventor, and tech wiz. She's often the team's voice of reason and a steadfast support to her friends on every mission.

Sage and Mina

These kind and hospitable villagers hosted Wu and Garmadon upon their unexpected arrival to the Valley of the Sphinx.

Shezada

This young, brave adventurer and treasure hunter has been trapped inside the pyramid like Wu and Garmadon. The brothers learn little about Shezada's past exploits or her origin, but her remarkable survival and combat skills save them from trouble many times.

Sphinx

This mighty creature has the head of a human and a body of a lion, often having mysterious powers. Most of Ninjago world's explorers believe that Sphinxes exist only in legends. The unlucky few who have actually met one wish it were true.

Spinjitzu

This is an ancient technique based on balance and rotation, where you tap your elemental energy while turning quickly. Developed by the First Spinjitzu Master long before time had a name, Spinjitzu is not only a martial art, but also a way of living. Mastering it is a life-long journey.

Wu

Wu is the other son of the First Spinjitzu Master, and little brother to Garmadon. After many years of mastering the art of Spinjitzu and the ways of the ninja, Wu shares his knowledge with his students— Lloyd, Kai, Cole, Jay, Zane, and Nya—to train them as ninja protectors of the world of Ninjago.

Zane

Brave and caring Zane is the Titanium Ninja, wielding the elemental power of ice. He is a Nindroid (ninja robot), created to protect those who cannot protect themselves.